MR. MUDDLE

by Roger Hargreaves

WORLD INTERNATIONAL

Poor Mr Muddle just couldn't get anything right.

Everything he did, everything he tried, everything he said was muddled.

Totally, utterly, completely, absolutely muddled!

Imagine, for instance, something as simple as hammering a nail into a wall.

Now what could get muddled with hammering a nail into a wall?

Mr Muddle could get it muddled!

And frequently did!

Imagine, for instance, something as simple as putting on your coat.

Now what could get muddled with putting on your coat?

Well, see for yourself.

Only Mr Muddle would put on his coat like that!

Imagine, for instance, something as simple as going for a walk.

Now what could get muddled about going for a walk?

Well, when your legs start walking one way and you start walking the other, that's a very muddly sort of a walk.

Poor Mr Muddle, walking one way and going another!

Now, you'd probably like to know where Mr Muddle lives.

In a house by the sea near a place called Seatown.

Mr Muddle's house was supposed to be in the country, but Mr Muddle (who built the house himself), had got the place muddled up!

Of course!

And you can tell that Mr Muddle had built the house himself, can't you?

This story starts one afternoon when Mr Muddle was having his breakfast.

Yes, we know you don't have breakfast in the afternoon, but you do if you get your mealtimes muddled up.

Mr Muddle was having bread and butter and jam and a cup of tea with milk and sugar.

He spread the butter on the table, and then spread the jam on the plate, and then poured the milk on the bread, and then filled the cup with sugar and then, poured the tea on the bread!

What a terrible muddly mixed-up breakfast!

That afternoon, after breakfast, he went for a walk down the beach near his house in order to work up an appetite for supper.

He met an old fisherman called George, whom he knew quite well.

"Good afternoon, Mr Muddle," said George.

"Good evening," replied Mr Muddle.

George smiled. "How would you like to come fishing with me?" he asked.

"Ooo, no please," replied Mr Muddle, eagerly.

"Help me push the boat out from the beach," called George.

"Rightho," said Mr Muddle, and pulled the boat further up on to the beach.

"Oh Mr Muddle," said George, and had to show Mr Muddle the difference between pulling and pushing.

However, eventually, somehow or other, they managed to get the boat out to sea.

"Now let's fish," said George, dropping a fishing line over the side of the boat.

"Rightho," said Mr Muddle, and dropped himself over the side of the boat!

SPLASH!

"Oh Mr Muddle," said George, again.

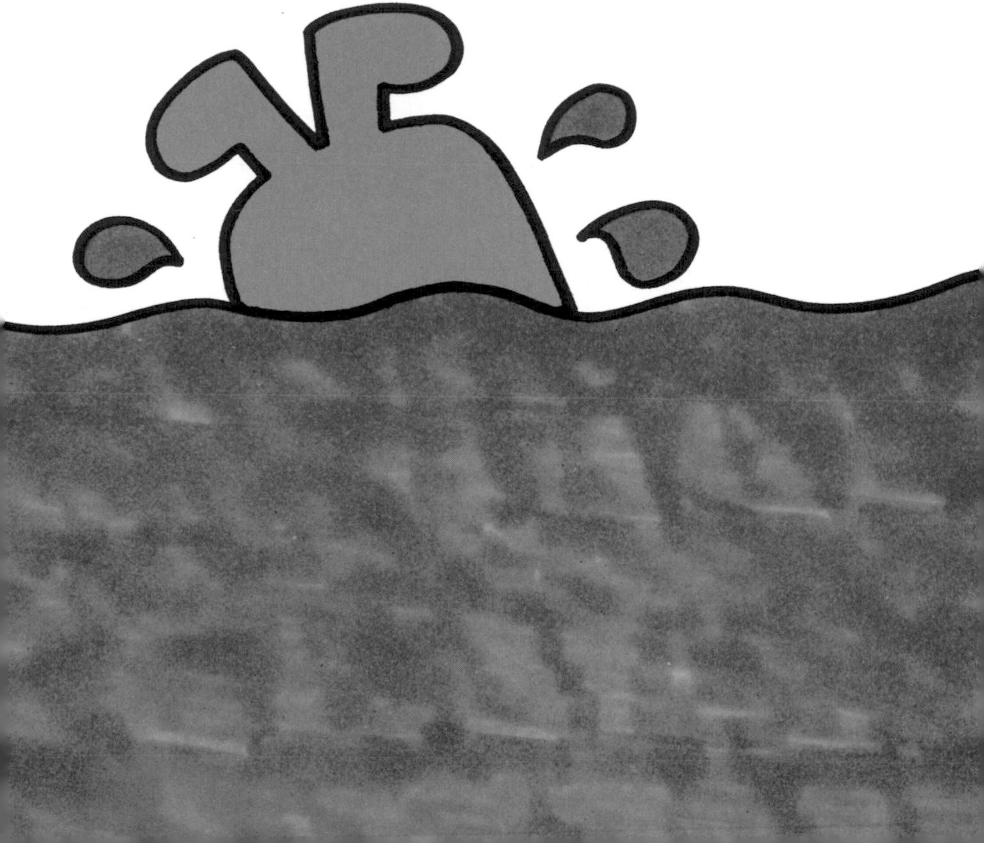

It wasn't any good, and they didn't catch any fish, and so they decided to go home before it became dark.

"Help me pull the boat up on to the beach," called George.

"Rightho," said Mr Muddle, and pushed the boat back into the water.

George was just about to say 'Oh Mr Muddle' again, when he had an idea.

He smiled to himself.

"Help me push the boat out into the sea," George called.

"Rightho," said Mr Muddle, and pulled the boat up on to the beach!

"Well done, Mr Muddle," said George.

Mr Muddle smiled a smile and went home.

George smiled a smile and went to tell everybody.

The following day, in Seatown, Mr Brick the builder asked Mr Muddle to hold his coat for him.

"Rightho," said Mr Muddle, and held his ladder for him – which is what Mr Brick really wanted.

"Well done, Mr Muddle," smiled Mr Brick, who'd been talking to George.

Mr Muddle was very pleased.

Then Mrs Scrub at the laundry asked Mr Muddle to pass her the soap.

"Rightho," said Mr Muddle, and passed her a clothes peg – which is what Mrs Scrub really wanted. "Well done, Mr Muddle," smiled Mrs Scrub, who'd also been talking to George.

Mr Muddle was extremely pleased.

And then Mr Black the coalman asked Mr Muddle to lift a sack of coal down from his lorry.

"Rightho," said Mr Muddle, and lifted a sack of coal up on to the lorry – which is what Mr Black really had wanted all along.

"Well done, Mr Muddle," smiled Mr Black.

George had talked to everybody!

Mr Muddle was delighted.

In fact, Mr Muddle was so delighted he decided to go home and cook himself a large meal to celebrate.

Roast turkey, and peas, and potatoes, and gravy!

He put the turkey in the cupboard to cook!

He peeled the peas!

He put the potatoes in the refrigerator to boil!

And then do you know what he did?

He tried to slice the gravy!!

Oh Mr Muddle!

Have you discovered the Little Miss books yet?
There are 30 to collect, and when you have
them all this is what you'll see!

Little Miss Giggles says,
"You'll laugh a lot with these little books!"

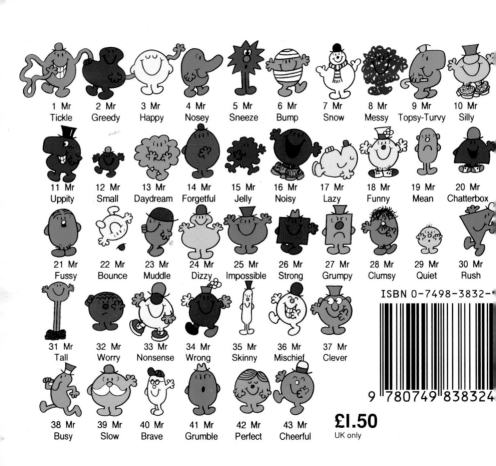

1 Mr Tickle
2 Mr Greedy
3 Mr Happy
4 Mr Nosey
5 Mr Sneeze
6 Mr Bump
7 Mr Snow
8 Mr Messy
9 Mr Topsy-Turvy
10 Mr Silly
11 Mr Uppity
12 Mr Small
13 Mr Daydream
14 Mr Forgetful
15 Mr Jelly
16 Mr Noisy
17 Mr Lazy
18 Mr Funny
19 Mr Mean
20 Mr Chatterbox
21 Mr Fussy
22 Mr Bounce
23 Mr Muddle
24 Mr Dizzy
25 Mr Impossible
26 Mr Strong
27 Mr Grumpy
28 Mr Clumsy
29 Mr Quiet
30 Mr Rush
31 Mr Tall
32 Mr Worry
33 Mr Nonsense
34 Mr Wrong
35 Mr Skinny
36 Mr Mischief
37 Mr Clever
38 Mr Busy
39 Mr Slow
40 Mr Brave
41 Mr Grumble
42 Mr Perfect
43 Mr Cheerful

ISBN 0-7498-3832-

9 780749 838324

£1.50
UK only